Charles Sotheran

Percy Bysshe Shelley

A Philosopher and Reformer

Charles Sotheran

Percy Bysshe Shelley
A Philosopher and Reformer

ISBN/EAN: 9783337296438

Printed in Europe, USA, Canada, Australia, Japan

Cover: Foto ©Raphael Reischuk / pixelio.de

More available books at **www.hansebooks.com**

AS A

PHILOSOPHER AND REFORMER.

BY

CHARLES SOTHERAN.

INCLUDING AN ORIGINAL SONNET

BY

CHARLES W. FREDERICKSON,

TOGETHER WITH

A PORTRAIT OF SHELLEY AND A VIEW OF HIS TOMB.

"Let us see the Truth, whatever that may be."—*Shelley.* 1822.

NEW YORK:

CHARLES P. SOMERBY, 139 EIGHTH STREET.

1876.

CHARLES WILLIAM FREDERICKSON,

OF NEW YORK.

DEAR FRIEND:

As in ancient times, none were allowed participation in the Higher Mysteries, without having proved their fitness for the reception of esoteric truth, so in these days only those seem to be permitted to breathe the hidden essence in Shelley, who have realized the acute phases of spirituality. Among the few who have enjoyed these bi-fold gifts, none have had more fortuitous experience than yourself, to whom I now take the liberty of dedicating this volume.

Yours fraternally,

CHARLES SOTHERAN.

December, 1875.

VIEW OF SHELLEY'S TOMB, IN THE PROTESTANT CEMETERY, AT ROME.
FROM A SKETCH BY A. J. STRUTT.

"To see the sun shining on its bright grass, and hear the whispering of the wind among the leaves of the trees, which have overgrown the tomb of Cestius, and the soil which is stirring in the sun-warm earth, and to mark the tombs, mostly of women and young children, who, buried there, we might, if we were to die, desire a sleep they seem to sleep."—SHELLEY.

In the Memory

OF

PERCY BYSSHE SHELLEY,

BY

CHARLES W. FREDERICKSON.

Amid the ruins of majestic Rome,
That told the story of its countless years,
I stood, and wondered by the silent dust
Of the "Eternal Child." Oh, Shelley !
To me it was not given to know thy face,
Save through the mirrored pages of thy works;
Those whisper'd words of wood and wave, are to mine ears,
Sweet as the music of ocean's roar, that breaks on sheltered shores.
Thy sterner words of Justice, Love and Truth,
Will to the struggling soul a beacon prove,
And barrier against the waves of tyranny and craft.
Then rest, " *Cor Cordium*," and though thy life
Was brief in point of years, its memory will outlive
The column'd monuments around thy tomb.

NEW YORK, *Nov.* 25, 1875.

MY DEAR SOTHERAN :—
  The copy of the lines on our Beloved Poet, which you requested, are entirely at your service—make what use of them you please.

    Yours, sincerely,

      C. W. FREDERICKSON.

PERCY BYSSHE SHELLEY, AS A PHILOSOPHER AND REFORMER.

A PAPER READ BEFORE THE NEW YORK LIBERAL CLUB,

ON FRIDAY, AUGUST 6TH, 1875.

" Let us see the Truth, whatever that may be."—SHELLEY, 1822.

Mr. Vice-President and Members of the Liberal Club:

" The Blood of the Martyr is the Seed of the Church." Persecution ever fails in accomplishing its desired ends, and as a rule lays the foundations broad and deep for the triumph of the objects of and principles inculcated by the persecuted.

Driven from their homes by fanatical tyranny, not permitted to worship as they thought fit, a band of noble and earnest, yet on some points mistaken men, were, a little over two hundred and fifty years ago, landed on this continent from the good ship "Mayflower." The "Pilgrim Fathers" were, in their native land, refused liberty of conscience and freedom of discussion; their apparent loss was our gain, for if it had not been for that despotism, and the corresponding re-action, which made those stern old zealots give to others many of the inalienable rights of liberty denied to themselves, you and I could not to-night perhaps be allowed to meet face to face, without fear, to discuss metaphysical and social questions in their broadest aspects, without the civil or theological powers intervening to close our mouths.

" Fragile in health and frame; of the purest habits in morals; full of devoted generosity and universal kindness; glowing with ardor to attain wisdom; resolved at every personal sacrifice to do right; burning with a desire for affection and sympathy," a boy-under-graduate of Oxford, described as of tall, delicate, and fragile figure, with large and lively eyes, with expressive, beautiful and feminine features, with head covered with long, brown hair, of gracefulness and simplicity of manner, the heir to a title and the representation of one of the most ancient English families, which numbered Sir Philip Sidney on its roll of illustrious names, just sixty-four years ago, and in this nineteenth century, for no licentiousness, violence, or dishonor, but, for his refusal to criminate himself or inculpate friends, was, without trial, expelled by learned divines from his university for writing an argumentative thesis, which, if it had been the work of some Greek philosopher, would have been hailed by his judges as a fine specimen of profound analytical abstruseness—for that expulsion are we the debtors to theological charity and tolerance for "Queen Mab."

Excommunicated by a mercenary and abject priesthood, cast off by a savage father, the admirer of that gloomy theology founded by the murderer of Michael Servetus, and charged by his jealous brother writers as one of the founders of a Satanic School, for neither immorality of life nor breach of the parental relation, but for heterodoxy to an expiring system of dogmatism, and for acting on and asserting the right of man to think and judge for himself, a father was to have two children torn from him, in the sacred name of law and justice, by the principal adviser of a dying madman, "Defender of the Faith, by Law Established," and by us despised as the self-willed tyrant, who lost America and poured out human blood like water to gratify his lust of power. By that Lord Chancellor whose cold, impassive statue has a place in Westminster Abbey, where Byron's was refused admittance, and whose memory, when that stone has crumbled into dust, will live as one who furnished an example for execrable tyranny over the parental tie, and that Lord Eldon whom an outraged father curses in imperishable verse :

> " By thy most impious hell, and all its terrors ;
> By all the grief, the madness and the guilt
> Of thine impostures, which must be *their* errors,
> That sand on which thy crumbling power is built ;
>
> *　　*　　*　　*　　*　　*
>
> By all the hate which checks a father's love ;
> By all the scorn which kills a father's care ;
> By those most impious hands that dared remove
> Nature's high bounds—by thee, and by despair.
>
> " Yes, the despair which bids a father groan,
> And cry, ' my children are no longer mine.

The blood within those veins may be mine own,
   But, tyrant, their polluted souls are thine.'
"I curse thee, though I hate thee not. O slave !
   If thou could'st quench the earth consuming hell
   Of which thou art a demon, on thy grave
   This curse should be a blessing. Fare thee well."

Sad as it is to contemplate any human being in his agony making use of such language to another ; and however much we may
sympathize with the poet, yet we cannot but have inwardly a
feeling of rejoicing ; for, if it had not been for this unheard of
villainy, we should probably never have had the other magnificent poetry and prose of Percy Bysshe Shelley composed during his self-imposed ostracism, and which furnish such glorious
thoughts for the philosopher, and keen trenchant weapons for
the reformer.

Have any of my hearers ever stood, in the calm of a summer
evening, in Shelley's native land, listening to the lovely warble
of the nightingale, making earth joyful with its unpremeditated
strains, and the woods re-echo with its melody? Or gazed up-
wards with anxious ken towards the skylark careering in the
"blue ether," far above this sublunary sphere of gross, sensual
earth, there straining after immortality, and

"Like a poet hidden,
   In the light of thought,
Singing hymns unbidden,
   Till the world is wrought
To sympathy with hopes and fears, it heeded not,"

pouring out such bursts of song as to make one almost worship
and credit the fables, taught in childhood at our mothers' knees, of
the angelic symphonies of heavenly choirs. Such was the poetry
of Shelley ; and as the music of the nightingale or the skylark
is far exceeding in excellence that of the other members of the
feathered kingdom, so does Shelley rank as a poet far above all
other poets, making even the poet of nature, the great Wordsworth himself, confess that Shelley was indeed the master
of harmonious verse in our modern literature. It is broadly laid
down in the Marvinian theory that all poets are insane.
I would much like to break a lance with the learned Professor
of Psychology and Medical Jurisprudence ; but as the overthrow
of this dogma does not come within the scope of my essay, I
would suggest to those who may have been influenced by that

paper to read Shelley's "Defence of Poetry." I shall quote two extracts therefrom, each pertinent to my subject. The first describes the function of the poet:

> "But poets, or those who imagine and express this indestructible order, are not only the authors of language and of music, of the dance, and architecture, and statuary, and painting; they are the institutors of laws, and the founders of civil society, and the inventors of the arts of life, and the teachers, who draw into a certain propinquity with the beautiful and the true, that partial apprehension of the agencies of the invisible world, which is called religion."

The other is in extension of the same idea, and concludes the essay:

> "Poets are the hierophants of an unapprehended inspiration; the mirrors of the gigantic shadows which futurity casts upon the present; the words which express what they understand not; the trumpets which sing to battle and feel not what they inspire; the influence which is moved not, but moves. Poets are the unacknowledged legislators of the world."

I have no hesitation in saying that for treating Shelley as a philosopher, I shall be attacked with great "positivism" by the disciples* of manufacturers of bran-new Brummagen philosophies dug out of Aristotelian and other depths to which are added new thoughts, not their own. The reason which David Masson offers in his "Recent British Philosophy" for placing Alfred Tennyson among the same class is equally applicable now:

> "To those who are too strongly possessed with our common habit of classifying writers into kinds, as historians, poets, scientific and speculative writers, and so on, it may seem strange to include Mr. Tennyson in this list. But as I have advisedly referred to Wordsworth as one of the representatives and powers of British philosophy in the age immediately past, so I advisedly

---

* If Diogenes or Socrates, leaving High Olympus and sweet converse with the immortals, were to condescend to visit New York some Friday evening, I am sadly afraid they would be astounded at many of their would-be brothers in philosophy. On seeing the travestie of ancient academies and groves where the schools used to congregate, the dialogues consisting of bald atheism under sheep's clothing to trap the unwary, and termed "The *Religion* of Humanity," of abuse and personality in lieu of argument, of buffoonery called wit, of airing pet hobbies alien to the subject instead of disputating, of shouting vulgar claptrap instead of rhetoric, etc. — I sadly fear these stout old Greeks, having power for the nonce, would, throwing philosophy to the dogs in a moment of paroxysmal indignation, despite physiognomies trained to resemble their own, have these fellows casked up in tubs without lanterns, but with the appropriate "snuffers," fit emblems of their faiths, and dropped far outside Sandy Hook. A proper finale to the vapid utterance made by one of these gentry that all "Reformers should be annihilated." Imagine Plato or Epicurus offering such a suggestion. O tempora! O mores!

named Tennyson as succeeding him in the same character. Though it is not power of speculative reason alone that consti-- tutes a poet, is it not felt that the worth of a poet essentially is measured by the depth and amount of his speculative reason? Even popularly, do we not speak of every great poet as the exponent of the spirit of his age? What else can this mean than that the philosophy of his age, its spirit and heart in relation to all the great elemental problems, find expression in his verse? Hence I ought to include other poets in this list, and more particularly Mr. Browning and Mrs. Browning, and the late Mr. Clough. But let the mention of Mr. Tennyson suggest such other names, and stand as a sufficient protest against our absurd habit of omitting such in a connection like the present. As if, forsooth, when a writer passed into verse, he were to be aban- doned as utterly out of calculable relationship to all on this side of the boundary, and no account were to be taken of his thoughts and doings, except in a kind of curious appendix at the end of the general register? What if philosophy, at a certain extreme range, and of a certain kind, tends of necessity to pass into poesy, and can hardly help being passionate and metrical? If so, might not the omission of poets, purely as being such, from a conspectus of the speculative writers of any time, lead to erroneous conclusions, by giving an undue prominence in the estimate of all such philosophizing as could most easily, by its nature, refrain from passionate or poetic expression? Thus, would philosophy, or one kind of philosophy in comparison with another, have seemed to had been in such a diminished condition in Britain about the year 1830, if critics had been in the habit of counting Wordsworth in the philosophic list as well as Coleridge, Mackintosh, Bentham, and James Mill? Was there not more of what you might call Spinozaism in Wordsworth than even in Coleridge, who spoke more of Spinoza? But that hardly needs all this justification, so far as Mr. Tennyson is concerned, of our reckoning *him* in the present list. He that would exclude In "Memoriam" (1850) and "Maud" (1855) from the conspectus of the philosophical literature of our time, has yet to learn what phi- losophy is. Whatever else "In Memoriam" may be, it is a manual for many of the latest hints and questions in British Meta- physics."

The soi-disant philosophers and classifiers of the sciences and arts who will not permit such poets as Shelley and Tennyson to be put in the category of philosophers, remind one very forcibly of the passage in Macbeth : "The earth has bubbles, as the water has, and these are of them !"

As a poet and not as a poet, as an acknowledged legislator for the race, as a philosopher, (a searcher after, or lover of wisdom) and as a political and social reformer, it is my intention to treat Shelley this evening, and having finished my prefatory remarks, will now regard him in those attributes which peculiarly should enshrine him in your hearts and mine.

The philosophical theories of advanced thinkers are always tinged with the reflex of that which called them forth, or impeded them in their development, consequently social bondage and the "anarch custom" being always present to Shelley, the great idea ever uppermost to him was that true happiness is only attainable in perfect freedom : the atrocious system of fagging, now almost extinct in the English Public Schools and the tyrannical venality of ushers, deeply impressed themselves on the mind of Shelley, and he tells us, in the beautiful lines to his wife, of the remembrance of his endeavors to overthrow these abominations having failed, of flying from "the harsh and grating strife of tyrants and of foes" and of the high and noble resolves which inspired him :

> "And then I clasp'd my hands, and look'd around ;
> But none were near to mock my streaming eyes,
> Which pour'd their warm drops on the sunny ground.
> So, without shame, I spake : ' I will be wise,
> And just, and free, and mild, if in me lies
> Such power ; for I grow weary to behold
> The selfish and the strong still tyrannize
> Without reproach or check.' I then controll'd
> My tears ; my heart grew calm ; and I was meek and bold.

> "And from that hour did I, with earnest thought,
> Heap knowledge from forbidden mines of lore ;
> Yet nothing that my tyrants knew or taught,
> I cared to learn ; but from that secret store
> Wrought linked armor for my soul, before
> It might walk forth, to war among mankind.
> Thus, power and hope were strengthen'd more and more
> Within me, till there came upon my mind
> A sense of loneliness, a thirst with which I pined."

The fruits born of this seed are discernible in every line of his works. While having all reverence for his college companions, Aristotle, Æschylus, and Demosthenes, his mind instinctively turns towards the deemed heretical works of the later French philosophers, D'Holbach, Condillac, La Place, Rousseau, the encyclopædists, and other members of that school. His intellect he furbishes with stores of logic and of chemistry, in which his greatest love was to experimentalize ; of botany and astronomy, in which he was more than a mere adept ; from Hume, too, whose essay on "Miracles," wrong as it is in the main on many important points, was one of the alphas of his creed—and with deep draughts from his great instructor, Plato, of whom he always spoke with the greatest adoration, as, for instance, in the preface to the Symposium :

"Plato is eminently the greatest among the Greek philosophers ; and from, or rather perhaps through him and his master, Socrates, have proceeded those emanations of moral and metaphysical knowledge, on which a long series and an incalculable variety of popular superstitions have sheltered their absurdities from the slow contempt of mankind."

It is desirable to call attention to the great minds from whom the student of the early part of this century could only cull his knowledge—he had no Spencer and no Mill, at whose feet to sit—he had in science none of the conclusions of Darwin, of Huxley, of Tyndall, of Murchison, of Lyell, to refer to, and yet I think, that the careful reader will, like myself, find prefigured in Shelley's works much of that of which the world is in full possession to-day, and which the mystical Occultists, Rosicrucians, and Cabalists have now, and have ever had, conjoined to a mysterious command over the active hidden material and spiritual powers in the infinite domain of nature.

The idea of the *Supreme Power* or *God*, as emanating from Shelley, is one of the most sublime to be found in the pages of metaphysical learning at the command of ordinary mortals. By many it may be considered only a vague pantheism ; yet, rightly regarded in a reconciliative spirit, it is of such an universal character as to harmonize with not only Deism, Theism and Polytheism, but even Atheistical Materialism. Listen to the following, which I select out of numerous examples, as a finger-post for others who seek the living springs of undefiled truth, as in Shelley:

"Whosoever is free from the contamination of luxury and license may go forth to the fields and to the woods, inhaling joyous renovation from the breath of Spring, and catch ing from the odors and sounds of autumn some diviner mood of sweetest sadness, which improves the softened heart. Whosoever is no deceiver and destroyer of his fellow-men— no liar, no flatterer, no murderer—may walk among his species, deriving, from the communion with all which they contain of beautiful or majestic, some intercourse with the Universal God. Whosoever has maintained with his own heart the strictest correspondence of confidence, who dares to examine and to estimate every imagination which suggests itself to his mind—whosoever is that which he designs to *become*, and only aspires to that which the divinity of his own nature shall consider and approve—he has already seen God."

Can any one cavil with these beautiful expressions, this out-pouring of genius ? If such there be, his heart and understand-ing must be sadly warped, any appeal would be in vain, for him the Veil of Isis could never be lifted.   After a careful study of Shelley's works I can find nothing to warrant the ex-ecration formerly levelled at his head, not even in the "Refuta-tion of Deism," that remarkable argument in the Socratic style between Eusebes and Theosophus in which, as in all his prose works, is displayed keen discernment, logical acuteness, and close analytical reasoning not surpassed by the greatest philo-sophers—most certainly his notions of God were not in unison with the current theological ideas, and it was this daring rebel-lion against the popular faith, the chief support of custom which caused all the trouble.   If ever he attempted to show the non-existence of Deity, his negation was solely directed against the gross human notions of a creative power, and *ergo* a succession of finite creative powers *ad infinitum*, or a Personal God who has only been acknowledged in the popular teachings as an autocratic tyrant, and as Shelley puts it in his own language :

"A venerable old man, seated on a throne of clouds, his breast the theatre of various passions, analogous to those of humanity, his will changeable and uncertain as that of an earthly king."

Not to be compared with the far different eternal and infinite.

"Spirit of Nature ! all sufficing power,
Necessity ! thou mother of the world !
Unlike the God of human error, thou
Requirest no prayers or praises, the caprice
Of man's weak will belongs no more to thee
Than do the changeful passions of his breast
To thy unvarying harmony."

And by this doctrine of necessity here apostrophised our philosopher instructs us in a lengthy statement of great clear-ness :

" We are taught that there is neither good nor evil in the universe, otherwise than as the events to which we apply these epithets have relation to our own peculiar mode of being. Still less than with the hypothesis of a personal God, will the doctrine of necessity accord with the belief of a future state of punishment. God made man such as he is, and then damned him for being so ; for to say that God was the author of all good, and man the author of all evil, is to say that one man made a straight line and a crooked one, and another man made the incongruity."

For you to better understand the exact position in which Shelley placed himself, it is elsewhere thus admirably expressed :

" The thoughts which the word ' God' suggest to the human mind are susceptible of as many variations as human minds themselves. The Stoic, the Platonist, and the Epicurean, the Polytheist, the Dualist, and the Trinitarian, differ entirely in their conceptions of its meaning. They agree only in considering it the most awful and most venerable of names, as a common term to express all of mystery, or majesty, or power, which the invisible world contains. And not only has every sect distinct conceptions of the application of this name, but scarcely two individuals of the same sect, which exercise in any degree the freedom of their judgment, or yield themselves with any candor of feeling to the influences of the visible world, find perfect coincidence of opinion to exist between them . . . . God is neither the Jupiter who sends rain upon the earth ; nor the Venus through whom all living things are produced ; nor the Vulcan who presides over the terrestrial element of fire ; nor the Vesta that preserves the light which is enshrined in the sun, the moon, and the stars. He is neither the Proteus nor the Pan of the material world. But the word ' God' unites all the attributes which these denominations contain and is the (inter-point) and over-ruling spirit of all the energy and wisdom included within the circle of existing things."

Of these attributes generally supposed to appertain to Deity, he writes :

" There is no attribute of God which is not either borrowed from the passions and powers of the human mind, or which is not a negation. Omniscience, omnipotence, omnipresence, infinity, immutability, incomprehensibility, and immateriality, are all words which designate properties and powers peculiar to organized beings, with the addition of negations, by which the idea of limitation is excluded."

There is no other writer, I think, who seems to grasp so clearly as Shelley the everlasting and immutable laws of Naturismus, or who believed so fully in the divine mission of man, and the religion of humanity. Ever soaring into the ideal, philosophizing by the aid of his emotional impulses, Shelley possessed, like all true Hermetists and Theosophists imbued with mysticism, a wonderful power of continued abstraction in the contemplation of the Supreme Power. His mentality, described by one of his critics as essentially Greek, "simple, not complex, imaginative rather than fanciful, abstract not concrete, intellectual not emotional," contributed its share to his belief in a pantheistic philosophy, making him find Supreme Intelligence permeated through the·

whole of infinite and interminable Nature. Regarding the universe as an abstract whole, he endorsed the fundamental metaphysics of Plato, and believed that "passing phenomena are types of eternal archetypes, embodiments of éternal realities."

Even if despite of my assertions to the contrary, there be those who still insist on the atheism of Shelley, they had better restudy the elementary axioms and learn to think—to those who imagine that there is but little difference between atheism and pantheism to the discredit of either, I would remind them that Bacon in his "Moral Essays," lays down as a principle that:—

"Atheism leaves to man reason, philosophy, nature, piety, laws, reputation and everything that can serve to conduct him to virtue; but superstition destroys all these, and erects itself into a tyranny over the understandings of men; hence atheism never disturbs the government, but renders man more clear-sighted, since he sees nothing beyond the boundaries of the present life."

In making use of this quotation do not let it be presumed that I wish to endorse Materialism; my desire is to add the authority of a great mind like that of the Elizabethan philosopher, to the fact that superstition is so hateful that even blank, bald atheism is preferable thereto. I should state that Bacon in extension of the extract I have quoted, speaking of this soul-destroying incubus on humanity observes that:—"A little philosophy inclineth men's minds to atheism; but depth in philosophy bringeth men's minds to religion."

No amount of mere reasoning, or argument *a priori* or *a posteriori*, can prove the existence of the Most High or destroy the same; in every breast is implanted an innate belief in Deity, the inner consciousness of the race, by the "Vox Dei" speaking within, has throughout all·time, the past and the present revelled in this sublimity, and will continue to do so in the future, notwithstanding the insane and insensate efforts of pseudo scientists or iconoclastic materialists—the brain and the heart must act in harmony to consolidate a pure philosophy, for mere intellect alone is an untrustworthy guide. By logic Whately proved apparently indisputably the non-existence of Napoleon Bonaparte, at the time when there was no doubt in any reasonable mind that he was actually living in the flesh, by the same means one can disprove one's own being, and so by this unsafe method have I frequently heard the God idea very learnedly overthrown. On such occasions I have simply taken the words of the logicians for what all their idle wind is worth—ZERO.

The Immortality of the Soul has ever been a subject of primary importance to all philosophers—the last dying efforts of Socrates, noblest of Greece's sons, as Plato has shown us in the Phædo, were expended in a discussion on the *pros* and *cons* of an argument in favor of a future life. Many of the highest intelligences since his day have been endeavoring to prove this satisfactorily without the aid of theological revelation. All mankind, from sage to peasant, from the most learned Brahmin on the banks of the Ganges to the untutored red Indian beside the Mississippi, has the question, "is there an existence after death," been approached with the most earnest hopes to solve as one of the greatest mysteries. Shelley devoted a vast amount of energy to the elucidation of this occult, yet overt, truth ; and in one place remarks :

"The desire to be forever as we are ; the reluctance to a violent and unexperienced change, which is common to all ; the animate and inanimate combinations of the universe, is, indeed, the secret persuasion which has (among other reasons) given birth to a belief in a future state."

Full well he knew, that independent of matter, there was a power, which has been denominated by some, Spirit ; by others, simply mind, force, or intelligence ; and by metaphysical philosophers, soul. If he approached the subject logically, as in his essay, "On a Future State," the *ignis fatuus* seems to escape him and be lost ; if poetically, with the innate voice which speaks within us all, ever present.

After close reasoning in the essay I have referred to, he arrived at the conclusion that even

"if it be proved that the world is ruled by a divine power, no inference can necessarily be drawn from that circumstance in favor of a future state,"

and that

"if a future state be clearly proved, does it follow that it will be a state of punishment or reward ?"

Then in extension of the same argument he urges :

"Sleep suspends many of the faculties of the vital and intellectual principle—drunkenness and disease will either temporarily or permanently derange them. Madness, or idiotcy, may utterly extinguish the most excellent and delicate of these powers. In old age the mind gradually withers ; and as it grew and strengthened with the body, so does it with the body sink into decrepitude."

He also considered that :

" It is probable that what we call thought is not an actual being, but no more than the relation between certain parts of that infinitely varied mass, of which the rest of the universe is composed. and which ceases to exist so soon as those parts change their position with regard to each other.   Thus color, and sound, and taste, and odor, exist only relatively."

Even granted that mind or thought be a part of, or in fact, the soul, then he asks in what manner it could be made a proof of its imperishability, as all that we see or know perishes and is changed.

Here then comes the query, "Have we existed before birth?" A difficult possibility to conceive of individual intelligence and if unprovable against the theory of existence after death.

He then winds up the whole by thinking that it is impossible that,

" we should continue to exist after death in some mode totally inconceivable to us at present."

and that only those who desire to be persuaded are persuaded.

This is but a rough outline of some of the principal features of his considerations on soul immortality from a logical basis, and which, after all, only constitute an argument, to which, and the thoughts presented therein, he did not necessarily bind himself.   There can be little doubt, independently of what I have quoted, that he did not believe in a future state as popularly accepted. Trelawney asked him on one occasion : " Do you believe in the immortality of the spirit?"   " Shelley's answer was unmistakable, " Certainly not ; how can I?   We know nothing ; we have no evidence." *

When we take Shelley from a poetical standpoint, or with the divine truism implanted by the Ain-soph clamoring within to his intelligence for expression, how confident he appears of a hereafter, as in the "Adonais," or in the following extract from an unpublished letter to his father-in-law, William Godwin, the property of my friend C. W. Frederickson, of New York, one of the most enthusiastic admirers of Shelley, and

* Those who desire to fully investigate Shelley's ideas on the immortality of the soul, and the existence, or nature, of Deity, will be amply repaid by reading W. M. Rossetti's admirable memoir of the poet, appended to the last two-volume London edition of his works.

who has been often known to pay more than the weight in gold for Shelleyana :

"With how many garlands we can beautify the tomb. If we begin betimes, we can learn to make the prospect of the grave the most seductive of human visions. By little and little we hive therein all the most pleasing of our dreams. Surely, if any spot in the world be sacred, it is that in which grief ceases, and for which, if the voice within our hearts mocks us not with an everlasting lie, we spring upon the untiring wings of a pangless and seraphic life—those whom we love around us—our nature, universal intelligence, our atmosphere, eternal love."

How exquisite these remarks and his description of a disembodied spirit :

" it stood
All beautiful in naked purity,
The perfect semblance of its bodily frame,
Instinct with inexpressible beauty and grace,
    Each stain of earthliness
Had passed away, it re-assumed
Its native dignity, and stood
    Immortal amid ruin."

It must appear impossible to any rational mind, that, with the full evidence before their eyes, materialists can attempt to claim Shelley as endorsing their doctrines, for even in the "Queen Mab," which has been considered by those not understanding it as a most atheistical poem, he speaks of—

"the remembrance
With which the happy spirit contemplates
Its well-spent pilgrimage on earth."

Positive dogmatists are tyrannically endeavoring to crush the belief in a soul, that All which makes the present life happy on earth, the hope of our heritage in a future state. To them the fact that the race from the dawn of history, and through the ages has knelt down in abnegation before this inscrutable truth is nothing. This glorious belief evolved from the primæval Cabala, taught in ancient Egypt, found contemporaneously in India, enunciated by scholarly Rabbis, ever present before the Chaldæan and Assyrian Magi, and laid down as axioms in the philosophical schools of Greece and Rome, not only to be discovered a fundamental in the Egyptian, the Hebraistic, the Brahminical, the Buddhistic, the Vedic, but also in all the sacred books of every nation, and handed down and perpetuated to these days as a sacred legacy from the past, by both Mohammed and Christ. This, the great co-mystery of all the ancient mysteries, shall remain ever present through all futurity like "the existing order of the Universe, or rather, of the *part of it known to us*," to use the phraseology of John Stuart Mill. Nations may rise and fall, theologies may flourish and decay, but this glorious and divine inheritance shall never pass away. Let pseudo-scientists avail themselves of stale and exploded arguments, and urge that there is no invisible world, and therefore no immortality for man, but honest scientists, like Professors Tait and Stewart, in the "Unseen Universe," will agree with the Illuminati: "in the position assumed by Swedenborg, and by the Spiritualists, according to which they look upon the invisible world not as something absolutely distinct from the visible universe, and absolutely unconnected with it, as is frequently thought to be the case, but rather as a universe that has some bond of union with the present;" and like Tyndall, will be obliged in abject humility to acknowledge, unlike the initiated occultist, that: "When we endeavor to pass from the phenomena of physics to those of thought, we meet a problem which transcends any conceivable expansion of the powers we now possess. We may think over the subject again and again—it eludes all intellectual presentation—we stand at length face to face with the incomprehensible."

Shelley was ever calling attention to the fact that either from ignorance or the casuistical sophistries of mal-interested teachers who have distorted the divine pristine truths for their own base ends, emanated superstition, the taint of all it looked upon; and with no unsparing hand he flagellated the professors of the numerous false faiths, bastardized from their original purity, which have in their decay, darkened the earth, and with all the force of his powerful pen, mightier than any sword, he ridiculed these gross theologies existant among men, as in the following:

"Barbarous and uncivilized nations have uniformly adored, under various names, a God of which themselves were the model : revengeful, blood-thirsty, groveling and capricious. The idol of a savage is a demon that delights in carnage. The steam of slaughter, the dissonance of groans, the flames of a desolated land, are the offerings which he deems acceptable, and his innumerable votaries throughout the world have made it a point of duty to worship him to his taste. The Phœnicians, the Druids and the Mexicans have immolated hundreds at the shrines of their divinity, and the high and holy name of God has been in all ages the watchword of the most unsparing massacres, the sanction of the most atrocious perfidies.'

Of the treatment Judaism, the foster mother of Christianity,

received at the poet's hands, I will now recite two examples.
To Moses, the Jehovah of the Hebrews is thus made to speak:

> " From an eternity of idleness
> I, God, awoke ; in seven days' toil made earth
> From nothing ; rested, and created man ;
> I placed him in a paradise, and there
> Planted the tree of evil, so that he
> Might eat and perish, and my soul procure
> Wherewith to sate its malice, and to turn
> Even like a heartless conqueror of the earth,
> All misery to my fame. The race of men
> Chosen to my honor, with impunity
> May sate the lusts *I* planted in their hearts.
> Here I command thee hence to lead them on,
> Until, with harden'd feet, their conquering troops
> Wade on the promised soil through woman's blood,
> And make my name be dreaded through the land,
> Yet ever-burning flame and ceaseless woe
> Shall be the doom of their eternal souls,
> With every soul on this ungrateful earth,
> Virtuous or vicious, weak or strong—even all
> Shall perish to fulfill the blind revenge
> (Which you to men call justice) of their God."

In another place Shelley is equally descriptive of the early
stages of Jewish history, and makes the following observations
on the building of the Temple of Jerusalem, which rearing high
its thousand golden domes to heaven, exposed its glory to the
face of day :

> "Oh ! many a widow, many an orphan cursed
> The building of that fane ; and many a father,
> Worn out with toil and slavery, implored
> The poor man's God to sweep it from the earth,
> And spare his children the detested task
> Of piling stone on stone, and poisoning
>   The choicest days of life,
>   To soothe a dotard's vanity.
> There an inhuman and uncultured race
> Howl'd hideous praises to their demon—God ;
> They rushed to war, tore from the mother's womb
> The unborn child—old age and infancy
> Promiscuous perished ; their victorious arms
> Left not a soul to breathe.   Oh ! they were fiends,
> And what was he who taught them that the God
> Of nature and benevolence had given
> A special sanction to the trade of blood ?
> His name and theirs are fading, and the tales
> Of this barbarian nation, which imposture
> Recites till terror credits, are pursuing
>   Itself into forgetfulness."

With the enlightenment of the present century in every department of knowledge, so has a corresponding degree of advancement been thrown on the science of history, which Shelley only partially apprehended. An enormous amount of new information is now to be gleaned from the writings of Ewald, Fergusson, Bünsen, Deutsch, Max Müller, Baring-Gould, Stanley, and other scholars of Orientation, which shows that the Hebrews, like every other nation, passed through the various phases of Nomadism and Pastoralism, to that of offensive and defensive war. The same as other races, they came through the usual steps in religious progress—Fetishism, Astrolatry, Polytheism and Monotheism. During phases in their history they participated in the various forms of tree and serpent, Phallic, or fire-worship. They had, as the Talmud, Targums, and the Old Testament show, a knowledge of the Egyptian or Chaldaic account of the creation and fall, the latter still to be seen on the walls of the temple of Osiris at Philæ. They had much knowledge of the Cabala, through their great prophet Moses, who was "learned in all the wisdom of the Egyptians," and, like Pythagoras, had been initiated into their mysteries, and who both imparted the knowledge in part to their compatriots, on which they both founded systems.

A great traveler, and most learned modern writer on Occultism, who claims, on good grounds, to have been received into the ancient branch of the Rosie Cross in the far East, Madame Helena P. de Blavatsky, imparts the following particulars: "The first Cabala in which a mortal man ever dared to explain the greatest mysteries of the universe, and show the keys to those masked doors in the ramparts of Nature, through which no mortal can ever pass without rousing dread sentries never seen upon this side her wall, was compiled by a certain Simeon Ben Jochai, who lived at the time of the second temple's destruction. Only about thirty years after the death of this renowned Cabalist, his MSS. and written explanations, which had till then remained in his possession as a most precious secret, were used by his son, Rabbi Elizzar, and other learned men. Making a compilation of the whole, they so produced the famous work called *Zohar* (God's splendor). This book proved an inexhaustible mine for all the subsequent Cabalists, their source of information and knowledge, and all more recent and genuine Cabalas were all more or less carefully copied from the former. Before that, all the mysterious doctrines had come down in an unbroken line of merely oral tradition as far back as man could trace himself on earth. They were scrupulously and jealously guarded by the wise men of Chaldea, India, Persia and Egypt, and passed from one initiate to another, in the same purity of form as when handed down to the first man by the angels, students of God's great Theosophic seminary.''

Many Free Thinkers, in their anxiety to crush everything belonging to Christianity, often forget that, in throwing aside the Hebrew records as utterly worthless, they are getting rid of one of the most ancient literatures in the world. They also do not remember the history of a peculiar nation, strangely preserved amid the fluctuations of time, the purity and excellence of the Book of Job, the Psalms, and others which I could name. They cast unmerited contempt on these compilations, when, at the same time, they will throw themselves, with almost Fetish reverence, and apparently rapt adoration, before the Institutes of Menu, the Bhagvat-Geeta, the morals of Chaoung-Fou-Tszee, the Zend-Avesta, the Rig-Veda, the Oracles of Zoroaster, the Book of the Dead, the Puranas, the Shastras, and the like.

Well may the Sons of Israel be proud of their ancient descent. They suffered through Christian persecutions uncomplainingly— the torture, the rack, the *auto-da-fe*—and yet they bowed their heads in submission to the will of Adonai. To-day they stand upright and united, as in olden times. They have gained the victory over the false disciples of the Nazarene, who, in days gone by, forgot their erudition, their medical knowledge, their commercial activity, and general culture. Pre-eminent in wealth and learning, they are found on the lecture-platform, in the fields of literature and science, in the councils of rulers, on the exchange, in the legislature—everywhere. When Greece and Rome were in their infancy, this extraordinary people was in middle age ; and when our Saxon forefathers were in the lowest stage of barbarism, they were in a state of high civilization ; and to-day, although scattered, they show a compact front, firmly knit in the bonds of brotherly love, a model for Christians. The great reform movement now agitating Judaism, as well as every other species of political and metaphysical thought, will eventually aid to consolidate all the races into one race—Humanity.

In order to make Christians prejudge Shelley it has been the
wont of theologians, as usual in fighting their antagonists, to
cry up a false issue, and to make their followers believe that he
was rather more than a mere hater of Jesus Christ, and of the
teachings of that religious and social reformer, in fact, that he
was an infidel of infidels.   To have no misconceptions—for it has
been stated that Shelley changed his views on Christ, which after
ten years' careful study of his writings, I utterly deny, it should
be thoroughly understood that he regarded this pious Israelite in
a duismal aspect—as Christ the Man, and as Christ the God.   I
must not, while here, forget that many advanced metaphysicians
agree that they cannot satisfactorily prove the historical existence of Christ, and that they have to winnow through a vast
amount of chaff to get at his presumed philosophy, and the facts
in his life, which like that of Buddha is wrapped up in tradi-
tional fable.

For the Man Christ, Jesus of Nazareth, the carpenter's carnate
son, the mystical Essene and occultist, Shelley exceeded in love
and reverence many of the most earnest Christians, and in no
theological writings can there be discovered such beautiful sen-
timents concerning the "The Regenerator of the World," and
the "Meek Reformer," of whom he speaks as contemplating that
mysterious principle called God, the fundamental of all good,
and the source of all happiness, as every true poet and philosopher must have done.   It is impossible to turn to any page of
his works, where, in speaking of Christ, he fails in this—he ex-
patiates with as great fervor as Renan, Seeley, or Strauss, on
Christ's exposing with earnest eloquence, like all true members
of the brotherhood of Illuminati, to which he belonged, the panic
fears and hateful superstitions which have enslaved mankind
for ages, and extols

"His extraordinary genius, the wide and rapid effects of his unexampled doctrines.
his invincible gentleness and benignity, (and) the devoted love borne to him by his
adherents."

For the God Christ, as depicted by the Sacerdotal order, he
had the greatest contempt.   It was impossible for a mind con-
stituted like his to tamely rest contented with the incredible
story forced on mankind's intelligence, that the Supreme
Power could or would for any wise purpose be transformed into a dove, and re-enact the mythical part of Jupiter with a

Christian Leda, the Jew carpenter's wife, Mary, under the disguise of a bird. Such a story and the theory on which it rests Shelley summarised as follows :

"According to this book, God created Satan, who, instigated by the impulses of his nature, contended with the Omnipotent for the throne of Heaven. After a contest for the empire, in which God was victorious, Satan was thrust into a pit of burning sulphur. On man's creation, God placed within his reach a tree whose fruit he forbade him to taste, on pain of death ; permitting Satan, at the same time, to employ all his artifice to persuade this innocent and wondering creature to transgress the fatal prohibition.

"The first man yielded to this temptation ; and to satisfy Divine Justice the whole of his posterity must have been eternally burned in hell, if God had not sent his only Son on earth, to save those few whose salvation had been foreseen and determined before the creation of the world."

The hero of this fabulous episode, beneath which a great truth lies hidden, the Christian Ahrimanes or Typhon, the Devil, as painted by Milton, he considered a moral being, far superior to the God depicted by the same author, and who, under the form of the second person of the Christian Trinity, Shelley tells us of coming humbly,

> "Veiling his horrible God-head in the shape
> Of man, scorn'd by the world, his name unheard,
> Save by the rabble of his native town,
> Even as a parish demagogue. He led
> The crowd ; he taught them justice, truth, and peace,
> In semblance ; but he lit within their souls
> The quenchless flame of zeal, and blest the sword
> He brought on earth to satiate with the blood
> Of truth and freedom his malignant soul."

Elsewhere, in extension of the same, he puts the accompanying words in the mouth of God the Father, to illustrate the doctrine of Christian Atonement :

> "I will beget a son, and he shall bear
> The sins of all the world ; he shall arise
> In an unnoticed corner of the earth,
> And he shall die upon a cross, and purge
> The universal crime ; so that the few
> On whom my grace descends, those who are marked
> As vessels to the honor of their God,
> May credit this strange sacrifice, and save
> Their souls alive. Millions shall live and die,
> Who ne'er shall call upon their Saviour's name,
> But unredeem'd go to the gaping grave ;
> Thousands shall deem it an old woman's tale,
> Such as the nurses frighten babes withal ;
> These, in a gulf of anguish and of flame,

Shall curse their reprobation endlessly,
Yet tenfold pangs shall force them to avow,
Even on their beds of torment, where they howl,
My honor and the justice of their doom.
What then avail their virtuous deeds, their thoughts
Of purity, with radiant genius bright,
Or lit with human reason's earthly ray?
Many are call'd but few will I elect."

The popular faith of Europe and America, which experience demonstrates to this age has, even as a means of reforming humanity, been a complete failure, Shelley correctly believed, had the same human foundation and origin as that of other revealed theologies—he sums up the proofs on which Christianity rests, miracles, prophecies, and martyrdoms, with great clearness; proves the absurdity of the doctrine of miracles, as taught by Christian writers, shows the falseness of the so-called prophecies, even granting the utmost warping of the real meaning of the Old Testament texts for Christian purposes, which he asserted were to be compared unfavorably with the oracles of Delphos, and points out that the Mohammedan dying for his prophet, or the Hindoo immolating himself under the wheels of Juggernaut could be cited equally as a proof of the divine origin of their faiths, as the reputed martyrdoms of Christians could of theirs.

The development of Christianity, which was really founded by Paul, was a subject to which Shelley devoted much attention—he tells us that

" The same means that have supported every other belief, have supported Christianity. War, imprisonment, assassination, and falsehood ; deeds of unexampled and incomparable atrocity, have made it what it is. The blood shed by the votaries of the God of mercy and peace, since the establishment of his religion, would probably suffice to drown all other sectaries now on the habitable globe. We derive from our ancestors a faith thus fostered and supported ; we quarrel, persecute, and hate, for its maintenance. Even under a government which, while it infringes the very right of thought and speech, boasts of permitting the liberty of the press, a man is pilloried and imprisoned because he is a deist, and no one raises his voice in the indignation of outraged humanity."

The numerical majority of Christians—the Greek and Roman Catholic—are as much pagans as their ancestors, the ancient Greeks and Romans were exoterically. And why? Simply because on the break-up of the Roman empire—like Mohammedanism afterwards, which was the natural reformation and revolution from Christian image-worship—Christianity, in a natural succession, and by fortuitous circumstances, took possession of the executive, and placed on the seat of power a Christian Byzantine emperor in lieu of a pagan. Basilicas, dedicated to Jupiter, Mercury, Adonis, Venus and the deities of High Olympus, were re-dedicated to God the Father, God the Son, God the Holy Ghost, the Virgin Mary, and the other saints (or gods) of the Christian Pantheon. Statues therein were re-christened, and the sacrificial altars were simply transferred for the use of the eucharistical sacrifice. The vestal virgins became nuns of the church; the *Sacerdotes*, her priests; the mysteries of Isis, her Agapæ. Her incense, her pictures, her image-worship, her holy water, her processions, and her prodigies, too, all came from the same source. Thus were the socialistic and communistic teachings, based on the Philoic-Essenism of the Reformer of Nazareth, paganized, prostituted, and entirely misrepresented. His life and labors were transformed from the natural into what was considered by the vulgar the supernatural, and all those who dared—like Hypatia, with thousands of other pious and noble ancients—to deny his divinity, were sacrificed to this new Moloch, set up by parricide Constantines, or adulterers of the Theodosius caste. Thus through the ages, has the race suffered under such murder, rapine, and lust, as never disgraced tolerant ancient heathendom in the interests of paganism, even as recently happened in Central America,* and would happen every-

---

* I refer to the abominable outrages perpetrated a few months ago at San Miguel, Panama, where popular preachers were forced by the ecclesiastical powers to foment rebellion by violently denouncing the State authorities, who had refused to allow a pastoral of the Christian Bishop of San Salvado-, hostile to the laws, to be read in the churches. Having been put into a state of frenzy by one Palacios, a canon of the cathedral, a fanatic mob revolted, liberated prisoners, murdered generals in command, massacred numbers of the best citizens, set fire to the city with kerosene, and destroyed over one million dollars' worth of property. After this theological revolt had been put down, passports, couched in the following terms, and sealed w.th the seal of the bishopric, were found on the bodies of some of these holy murderers:

"PETER.—Open to the bearer the gates of heaven, who has died for religion.
(Signed), GEORGE, Bishop of San Salvador."

Similar attempts were made by the Christian hierarchy in Brazil against the Masonic body; but, fortunately, the emperor, a liberal and an enlightened savant, crushed the attempt under foot, and unmistakably proved, to the satisfaction of humanity, that he was not to be transformed into a nineteenth century Charles the Ninth or Philip the Second, and act the cat's paw for Pio Nono, ex-carbonari and recusant mason, to wreak his vengeance on the brethren whom he had betrayed.

where else, if priestcraft had the power to act without restraint, so that, as Shelley says,

> " Earth groans beneath religion's iron age,
> And priests dare babble of a God of Peace—
> Even whilst their hands are red with guiltless blood,
> Murdering the while, uprooting every germ
> Of truth, exterminating, spoiling all,
> Making the earth a slaughter-house."

To those who will look down the ages, I would ask, is this picture overdrawn? and further, to remember that in Shelley's own words:

> " Eleven millions of men, women and children have been killed in battle, butchered in their sleep, burned to death at public festivals of sacrifice, poisoned, tortured, assassinated and pillaged in the spirit of the religion of peace, and for the glory of the most merciful God."

Is it amazing that he should have written such a "highly wrought and admirably sustained" tragedy as the "Cenci," founded on facts, and which has been deemed by competent critics the first since Shakspeare—that he should have brought forward, with vivid delineation, the crimes of the priesthood—and that he should have made us remember the terrors of the bloody wars on heretics and heathen, in words such as these:

> "Yes! I have seen God's worshippers unsheathe
> The sword of His revenge, when grace descended,
> Confirming all unnatural impulses,
> To sanctify their desolating deeds;
> And frantic priests wave the ill-omen'd cross
> O'er the unhappy earth; then shone the sun
> On showers of gore from the upflashing steel
> Of safe assassination, and all crime
> Made stingless by the spirits of the Lord.
> And blood-red rainbows canopied the land.
> Spirit! no year of my eventful being
> Has pass'd unstain'd by crime and misery,
> Which flows from God's own faith. I've marked his slaves
> With tongues whose lies are venomous, beguile
> The insensate mob, and whilst one hand was red
> With murder, feign to stretch the other out
> For brotherhood and peace; and that they now
> Babble of love and mercy, whilst their deeds
> Are marked with all the narrowness and crime
> That freedom's young arm dare not yet chastise?"

Protestant Christians may urge that all this is not Christianity; if it be not—for it is the record of the Church—I would ask, what is? and where shall we find the history of Christiani-

ty for the fifteen centuries before Luther's time ? and where, to-
day ?   Their predecessors plucked the plumage from the dying
bird of mythology, as they, themselves, have robbed the liberal
orchard of all its choicest fruits and palmed them off as of their
own growth.   Protestants would not, I dare say, now counte-
nance the persecutions of the past, but yet, I would tell them
that their Protestantism has been a great mistake ; and that,
at this moment, there is no unity among the opposers of Catholicism, who are split into a thousand sects, wrangling for
superiority, like wolves over offal ; and that their churches
are gradually converging toward Rationalism on the one
hand, and Catholic Sacerdotalism on the other ; in regard to
which last, the Historical Roman Church—the only Christian
body which presents a solid phalanx—one must not be too iconoclastic, remembering that, in the monastic houses and great
ecclesiastical libraries we have had conserved for us, although,
perchance by accident, the records of all the philosophy, all
the jurisprudence, all the polity, all the literature, and all the
civilization of ancient Greece and Rome, that remained from
the Alexandrian library and pre-Christian times—the mediæval
clerics were the great conservators of knowledge, which we in-
herit directly from Europe ; and we should be, therefore,
grateful   to   them   equally   with   Mohammedanism,   from
which we received, through the Crusaders and the Moors, the
basis of nearly all science and luxury, from Asia.   There were,
undoubtedly, many bad popes, men as bad as the incestuous,
and, according to the recent dogma, the infallible Alexander
Borgia ; priests who are not all vile, but many nobler than their
system, acknowledge this with regret, and among whom there
are some whom I can reverence, such as John Henry Newman, for
instance, whose life would favorably compare with that of
Shelley, or any liberal.   There have been popes, also, whose
lives have been as pure, as disinterested, and as virtuous as that
of any stoic or epicurean.   We owe much to Sixtus the Fifth,
founder of the Vatican Library, and would-be regenerator of
order in his temporal dominions ; to Leo the Great, whose pat-
ronage of the arts has sent us down the wondrous statuary, paint-
ing, and works of genius, which are the admiration of the world ;
and to Hildebrand, who brought together, in one harmonious
whole, the struggling elements of European society.   It is well

to note, too, in order that I may not be misunderstood, that
Catholicism is better than savage Fetishism, and Rationalism in degree superior to either ; and, further, that Liberalism
should only war with evil principles, and not with men whom
they are generally the exponents of ignorantly, and to the best
of their knowledge.   Comtism * acknowledges the fact that
Christianity was not simply a mere advance on, but where we
shall only find the civilization of Europe as it was during mediæval
times, and recognizes this most strongly, by placing over fifty
of these great geniuses and luminaries, popes, bishops, and
saints of the Catholic Church, in the Comtist Calendar, under
the sixth and seventh months dedicated to St. Paul or Catholicism, and Charlemagne or Feudal Civilization respectively.   We
should thank the followers of Comte for thus bringing to our
notice what we might be liable to occasionally forget in our
bigotry and frequent over-anxiety.

In popularizing terms wrongly, lies much mischief.   If the
misapplied term Christianity, signify the current notion, zeal
for truth, the good of mankind, and active virtue or Christism,
the reputed precepts of Christ, then Shelley taught that ethical
system, and the so-called Christian world which persecuted him,
the opposite.

No one believed, better than Shelley, in the necessity of con-
tinuity, and that all theological systems are a portion of the development of Humanity.

It should likewise be remembered, that even in the grossest
superstition, as in the highest belief, the underlying aspiration,
veiled perhaps, under some beautiful myth, is a straining after
the pure and the good, and, as Shelley puts it :

> "All original religions are allegorical, or susceptible of allegory, and, like Janus,
> have a double face of false and true."

It should also be considered, that it is better not to interfere
with the faith of the ignorant, but let them remain in an exoteric

---

* Comtism, or Positivism is that casuistical system of modern Atheism, founded by
Auguste Comte, the Ignatius Loyola of Materialism, and which that learned pantarchical
madman strung together in Esquirol's lunatic asylum.   It is an insidious philosophy, full
of Jesuistry, and teaches a *soi-disant* Religion which is Ir-religion, a pseudo-God, which
has no conceivable existence, and an impossible immortality of the soul, ignoring a
future state.   The present crusade of Comtism in our midst, with false colors flying can
be justly compared to that of St. Francois Xavier in Hindostan.

condition, until they are properly developed by sufficient education and consequent intelligence. It is just as much the duty of advanced thinkers not to tamper with the beliefs of men who are in an early stage of progress, as it is not to put a flaming torch in the possession of a lunatic, or a razor in the hands of a child.

Shelley, in his philosophy, accepted all this, with the full consciousness that in the end truth would prevail—he yearned for the time when priest-led slaves would

> " Cease to proclaim that man
> Inherits vice and misery, when force
> And falsehood hang even o'er the cradled babe,
> Stifling with rudest grasp all natural good,"

and for that epoch when "the Mohammedan, the Jew, the Christian, the Deist, and the Atheist will live together in one community, equally sharing the benefits which arise from its associations, and united in the bonds of charity and brotherly love."

With Shelley we can turn with delight to the gospels of the future, as of the ancient past; and the ramifications of the Trinity of a truly Rational Religion, Nature, Science, and Art, where we have, instead of idle prayers, addressed to gross material idols, or the impossible entities hitherto depicted in theological systems, a feeling of real satisfaction in learning how to live rather than to die, and in practicing virtue and benevolence for their own sakes, than for improbable rewards in the unsatisfactory hereafter, enunciated from the theological platform.

Like a true religionist, Shelley tells us that aspirations to "Madre Natura," like the following, should be poured out in silent, grateful communion with Omnipresence, and not in temples made by hands:

> Spirit of Nature ! here !
> In this interminable wilderness
> Of worlds, at whose immensity
> Even soaring fancy staggers,
> Here is thy fitting temple.
> Yet not the slightest leaf
> That quivers to the passing breeze
> Is less instinct with thee ;
> Yet not the meanest worm
> That lurks in graves, and fattens on the dead
> Less shares thy eternal breath.

Spirit of Nature ! thou !
Imperishable as this scene,
Here is thy fitting temple.

From such a soul-inspiring altar should praises like these be raised, and with what sacred feeling would the pure worshipper revel ''where spirits live and dream—where all that is sweet in sound, or pure in vision floats on the air, or passes dimly before the sight,'' for as the late Professor J. G. Hoyt, in his essay on Shelley beautifully points out—''To him everything was God, and God was everything. Every place was peopled with forms of beauty and animated with living intelligences. Hills and valleys, forests and fountains, were each thronged with presiding deities—bright effluences from the Divinity that stirred within, and shone above the whole.''

In leaving the first portion of my paper, I will make the following quotation from a remarkable article on Shelley in the pages of the *National Magazine*, which all minds unshackled, and free from prejudice, must acknowledge to be correct in the main, and which admirably sums up his efforts in metaphysical philosophy. Our attention is called to the fact that we discover in all Shelley's writings ''a freer and purer development of what is best and noblest in ourselves. We are taught in it to love all living and lifeless things, with which in the material and moral universe we are surrounded—we are taught to love the wisdom and goodness and majesty of the Almighty, for we are taught to love the universe, his symbol and visible exponent. God has given two books for the study and instruction of mankind ; the book of revelation and the book of nature. In one at least of these was Shelley deeply versed, and in this one he has given admirable lessons to his fellow-men. Throughout his writings, every thought and every feeling is subdued and chastened by a spirit of unutterable and boundless love. The poet meets us on the common ground of a disinterested humanity, and he teaches us to hold an earnest faith in the worth and the intrinsic Godliness of the soul. He tells us—he makes us feel that there is nothing higher than human hope, nothing deeper than the human heart ; he exhorts us to labor devotedly in the great and good work of the advancement of human virtue and happiness, and stimulates us

' To love and bear—to hope till hope creates
From its own wreck the thing it contemplates.' ''

It is observed by Shelley that

" The exertions of Locke, Hume, Gibbon, Voltaire, Rousseau, and their disciples in favor of oppressed and deluded humanity, are entitled to the gratitude of mankind. Yet it is easy to calculate the degree of moral and intellectual improvement which the world would have exhibited, had they never lived. A little more nonsense would have been talked for a century or two ; and perhaps a few more men, women and children burnt as heretics. We might not at this moment have been congratulating each other on the abolition of the Inquisition in Spain."

The vast impetus, which these extraordinary geniuses gave to freedom in metaphysical strongholds, led to a corresponding degree of liberty in the political and social relations. Shelley was not one who

" beheld the wce
In which mankind was bound, and deem'd that fate
Which made them abject, would preserve them so."

but on the contrary was aware of the progressive character of the race, and threw himself with all his heart and soul into the cause of Republicanism, and never slackened in his efforts till death took him from his work. His noblest endeavors were directed toward the cause of suffering humanity, crushed under the weight of despotism ; and his tuneful lyre was ever struck in behalf of the Goddess of Freedom, to whom, in that soul inspiring " Ode to Liberty," he offers chaplets of the most glorious verse to rouse the nations from their apathy. He has given us his reflections on the English Revolution, when Cromwell crushed royalty under his feet in the person of the tyrant Charles Stuart, and which, notwithstanding, rose again to befoul, in the profligacy and debauchery of the second Carolian epoch ; on the French Revolution, when an intelligent people drove out a brood of vampires, who had drained the blood of France too long, to be replaced by atrocious demagogues, hateful priest-ridden Bourbons and a Napoleon Bonaparte, the wholesale Jaffa poisoner, on whose death Shelley wrote lines pregnant with republican feelings :

" I hated thee, fallen tyrant ! I did groan
To think that a most ambitious slave,
Like thou, shouldst dance and revel on the grave
Of Liberty. Thou mightst have built thy throne
Where it had stood even now ; thou didst prefer
A frail and bloody pomp, which time has swept
In fragments towards oblivion. Massacre,
For this I pray'd would on thy sleep have crept,
Treason and Slavery, Rapine, Fear and Lust,

And stifled thee, their minister. I know
Too late, since thou and France are in the dust,
That virtue owns a more eternal foe
Than force or fraud ; old custom, legal crime,
And bloody Faith, the foulest birth of time."

With full knowledge of all this, he hopefully looked with loving eyes toward this side of the Atlantic, to your magnificent constitution and model Republic, built on the consolidated masonic bases of Liberty, Equality, and Fraternity, as did also the mass of my compatriots, who, suffering under a more intolerant despotism, and unable to help themselves, had no hand or voice in the attempted tyranny, from which your forefathers properly rebelled one hundred years age.

In "Hellas" we find Shelley advocating the cause of Greece, and it is believed, that that poem assisted his friend Byron in the determination to wield his sword in the cause of Grecian Liberty. "The Revolt of Islam," his most mystical work, next to his early effort, " St. Irvyne, or the Rosicrucian," is full of the most majestic and sympathetic thoughts, and underlying its weirdness we have all those elements "which essentially compose a poem in the cause of a liberal and comprehensive morality, and with the view of kindling in the bosom of his readers a virtuous enthusiasm for those doctrines of liberty and justice, that faith and hope in something good, which neither violence, nor misrepresentation, nor prejudice, nor the continual presence and pressure of evil, can ever totally extinguish among mankind."

Can we wonder that Shelley could be else than Republican when he regarded what Thackeray afterward summed up with biting irony, the record of the reigning house of Great Britain, the mad Guelph *Defenders of the Christian Faith* (?), the results of whose labors have been corroborated by Greville and recent writers ?

To what a line of monarchs, was Shelley called upon to give allegiance and prostrate himself before, and can we be astonished that he thus describes the state these abominable Hanoverians had "England in 1819 :"

"An old, mad, blind, despised and dying king,—
Princes the dregs of their dull race who flow
Through public scorn, mud from a muddy spring,—
Rulers who neither see, nor feel, nor know,
But leech-like to their fainting country cling,
Till they drop blind in blood without a blow,—

> A people starved and stabbed in untilled field,—
>   An army which liberticide and prey
> Make as a two-edged sword to all who wield,—
>   Golden and sanguine laws which tempt and slay—
> Religion Christless, Godless, a book sealed,—
> A Senate—time's worst statute unrepealed,—
>   Are graves from which a glorious phantom may
> Burst to illumine our tempestuous day?"

To aid Republicanism, he threw himself with fervor into the cause of the unhappy Caroline of Brunswick; and on her account he wrote "God Save the Queen," in imitation of the British national anthem, and the satirical piece entitled "Swellfoot, the Tyrant." In the following words he attacked the prime minister, Lord Castleragh, whose reactionary counsels were transforming England into a state analogous to that of Russia to-day:

> "Then trample and dance, thou oppressor,
>   For thy victim is no redressor!
>   Thou art sole lord and possessor
> Of her corpses, and clods and abortions—they pave
>   Thy path to a grave.

For the Lord Chancellor, Eldon, his hatred was intense; for, in addition to the crime of robbing him of his children, this occupant of the wool-sack, had made the seat of justice an appanage for his lust of wealth and power. I have already quoted some verses on this renowned lawyer, and will now present you with two others bearing on the same subject:

> "Next came Fraud, and he had on,
>   Like Lord Eldon, an ermine gown;
>   His big tears (for he wept well)
>   Turned to mill stones as they fell;

> "And *the little children*, who
>   Round his feet played to and fro,
>   Thinking every tear a gem,
>   Had their brains knocked out by them."

In *Queen Mab*, Shelley has presented us with an unmistakable portraiture of the "First Gentleman in Europe;" and in the following lines, which I have taken from this poem, I have chosen two extracts, descriptive of the origin of political despotism, and the reason of its continuance:

> "Whence, thinkest thou, kings and parasites arose?
> Whence that unnatural line of drones, who heap
> Toil and unvanquishable penury

> On those who build their palaces, and bring
>   Their daily bread? From vice, black, loathsome vice,
> From rapine, madness, treachery and wrong ;
> From all that genders misery, and makes
> Of earth this thorny wilderness ; from lust,
> Revenge and murder."
>
>   *   *   *   *   *
>
> " Nature rejects the monarch, not the man ;
>   The subject, not the citizen ; for kings
> And subjects, mutual foes, forever play
> A losing game into each other's hands,
> Whose stakes are vice and misery. The man
> Of virtuous soul commands not nor obeys.
> Power, like a desolating pestilence,
> Pollutes whate'er it touches ; and obedience,
> Bane of all genius, virtue, freedom, truth,
> Makes slaves of men, and of the human frame
> A mechanized automaton."

Shelley believed in reformation, not revolution ; and in the "Revolt of Islam" and his Irish pamphlets, we find him advocating a bloodless revolution, except where force was used, and then force for force, if compromise were hopeless. His idea was ever the foundation of political systems founded on that of this country, or on the ancient Greek Republic. He says :

> " The study of modern history is the study of kings, financiers, statesmen, and priests. The history of ancient Greece is the study of legislators, philosophers, and poets ; it is the history of men compared with the history of titles. What the Greeks were was a reality, not a promise. And what we are and hope to be is derived, as it were, from the influence of these glorious generations."

Hoping almost against hope for the regeneration of his country, he submitted to the people of England a proposal for putting to the vote the great reform question, which was filling the public mind ; but he was conscious that in the then unprepared state of public knowledge and feeling, universal suffrage was fraught with peril, and remarks that although

> " A pure republic may be shown, by inferences the most obvious and irresistible, to be that system of social order the fittest to produce the happiness and promote the genuine eminence of man. Yet nothing can less consist with reason, or afford smaller hopes of any beneficial issue, than the plan which should abolish the regal and the aristocratical branches of our constitution, before the public mind, through many gradations of improvement, shall have arrived at the maturity which shall disregard these symbols of its childhood."

An essay has come down to us (unhappily unfinished), in which he argues in favor of "Government by Juries." It is but a fragment, and yet it shows us that his mind was ever in search of the right solution of the question of proper legislation for the masses. William Pitt, with enemies on every side, publicly acknowledged the extraordinary genius which impelled the American revolution, and admired the constitution of this country, as well as the masterly character of the "Declaration of Independence." In unstinted praise does he speak of the learning and remarkable public spirit of the signers. With equal praise, I am confident, everyone must eulogize the "Declaration of Rights," compiled by Shelley, which he put before his countrymen sixty-three years ago. Therein he has given the whole of his conception of the correct theory of government, and it cannot fail to be read by advanced minds with feelings of genuine pleasure.

The race has suffered through its long martyrdom with the horrors of war. One tyrant after another, to aid his accursed ambition or revenge his spite upon a brother monarch, has cursed the unhappy earth and humanity with the terrors of long-continued devastation and bloodshed. With burning pen has Shelley depicted war in its most hideous aspects, and by most beautiful comparisons has he shown us the sublimity of peace. He points out, that

> " War is the statesman's game, the priest's delight,
> The lawyer's jest, the hired assass.n's trade."

He repudiates the notion that man, if left free, would wantonly heap ruin, vice, or slavery, or curse his species with the withering blight of war ; and he shows us how

> " Kings, priests, and statesmen blast the human flower,
> Even in its tender bud ; their influence darts
> Like subtle poison through the bloodless veins
> Of desolate society. The child,
> Ere he can lisp his mother's sacred name,
> Swells with the unnatural pride of crime, and lifts
> His baby sword even in a hero's mood.
> This infant arm becomes the bloodiest scourge
> Of devastated earth : whilst specious names,
> Learnt in soft childhood's unsuspecting hour,
> Serve as the sophisms with which manhood dims
> Bright reason's ray, and sanctifies the sword
> Upraised to shed a brother's innocent blood."

In other places he seems to prophetically point out what this generation appears to comprehend—the judiciousness of arbitration—which in the future will be the true panacea for this frightful affliction of humanity.

To the current Irish questions Shelley devoted much of his time, and took up his residence in Dublin, to aid the independence of Ireland, which might, under proper treatment, have been made one of the brightest spots in the British Dominions; but the inhabitants of which, owing to centuries of English misrule and oppression, had, in certain parts, fallen into a condition not much superior to that of those of Central Africa. When we contemplate what Ireland was before the Norman and Saxon had set their feet there, the most prejudiced antagonist of the Celtic race cannot but be astonished at the picture presented to us after their usurpation. When Saxondom was in a state of barbarism, this branch of the Celts was civilized. Aldfred, king of the Northumbrian Saxons, has given us the experiences of a Saxon in Ireland over a thousand years ago. In a poem of his own composing, he tells us that he found "noble, prosperous sages," "learning, wisdom, welcome, and protection," "kings, queens, and royal bards, in every species of poetry well skilled. Happiness, comfort, and pleasure," the people "famed for justice, hospitality, lasting vigor, fame," and "long blooming beauty, hereditary vigor"— and the monarch concludes his really curious account by saying:

> "I found in the fair, surfaced Leinster,
> From Dublin to Slewmargy,
> Long-living men, health, prosperity,
> Bravery, hardihood and traffic.
>
> I found from Ara to Gle,
> In the rich country of Ossory,
> Sweet fruit, strict jurisdiction,
> Men of truth, chess-playing.
>
> I found in the great fortress of Meath,
> Valor, hospitality, and truth,
> Bravery, purity, and mirth--
> The protection of all Ireland.
>
> I found the aged of strict morals,
> The historians recording truth—
> Each good, each benefit that I have sung,
> In Ireland I have seen."

Such is the statement of King Aldfred, and the Venerable Bede informs us that in Ireland, Saxons and other foreigners were "hospitably received, entertained and educated, furnished with books," etc., all gratuitously.

Up to the middle of the sixteenth century, I find, after careful study in the Leabhar-Gabhala, the Annals of the Four Masters, of Clonmacnoise, of Loch Cé, and other historical records, the same continued apparent prosperity, but after the English took possession of the larger portion of the country, only the records of anarchy, despotism, and misery. Before the Reformation, or so long as the English settlers remained within the pale, Ireland had been as happy as Ultramontanism would allow, but from the accession of Elizabeth and the consequent attempted enforcement of a new theology, against the wishes of the people, a fearful succession of despotism is revealed. To force Protestantism on the Irish, Catholicism was put down by the most stringent laws—the torture chamber never empty, the scaffold rarely free from executions, the seaports closed, and manufactures forbidden to be exported ; "black laws" of a most iniquitous character, exceeding in ingenuity the devices of Tilly or Torquemada, placed on the statute book. The punishment for being a recusant Catholic, or Papist, was death, and it is a known fact that one Protestant commander, Sir William Cole, of Fermanagh, made his soldiers massacre in a short period " seven thousand of the vulgar sort," as Borlase informs us. Elsewhere the English behaved in the same manner, and on the authority of Bishop Moran it is asserted that the Puritans of the North shot down Catholics as wild beasts, and made it their business "to imbrue their swords in the hearts' blood of the male children." Mr. and Mrs. S. C. Hall, in their valuable work on Ireland, state that the possessors of the whole province of Ulster were driven out under pain of mortal punishment from their homes and lands, without roof over their heads, to be pent up in the most barren portion of Connaught, where to pass a certain boundary line was instant death without trial, and where it was commonly said, "There is not wood enough to hang a man, water enough to drown him, nor earth enough to bury him." One hundred thousand Catholics were sold as slaves to the West Indian and North American planters by the public authority of the Cromwellian government. Such was the way these Christians showed their love for their fellow Christians, and can it be wondered that ever since then there

has been one continual succession of uprisings in that most unhappy country ? As the sinew of Ireland's people in this country
were driven by necessity, fleeing from the terrors of starvation
and insufficient existence at home, so were the best of the race
in the two previous centuries necessitated to fly to the European
continent, where we find them enrolled, for instance, in the
service of the King of France, and having revenge on their oppressors on the field of Fontenoy. Elsewhere in every country
of Europe do we discover them or their descendants in the front
ranks, and at the helm of affairs—in Spain, O'Donnell and
Prim ; in France, Mac Mahon and Lally Tollendal ; in Austria,
O'Taafe and Maguire.

When Shelley arrived in Dublin in 1812, he soon found himself joined to the body of the Repeal party, which was endeavoring to obtain back the parliament which had been stolen from
them by British gold, less than a quarter of a century before,
and to have the Catholic Emancipation Bill made law. He
published two remarkable political pamphlets, in those days
the only mode by which a statesman could appeal to the people,
in which it may be noticed how well he could write in a popular style, to effectually serve a purpose. They also prove
his enthusiasm for the liberty of discussion, and how, although
he was always willing to treat on politics alone, he was pre-
occupied with metaphysical questions which continually crop
out.

In the first, which he called *An Address to the Irish People*,
and wrote during the first week of his residence in Ireland,
he commences by eulogizing the Irish, explains to them that
all religions are good which make men good, and shows that,
being neither Protestant nor Catholic, he can offer the olive
branch to each. He then points out the weak spots in each
other's conduct in the past, the necessity of toleration, and the
crime of persecution—how different this was to what Christ
taught !

He endeavors to prove that arms should not be used—that
the French Revolution, although undertaken with the best intentions, ended badly because force was employed. He recom-
mends sobriety, regularity and thought; for the Irish not to
appeal to bloodshed, but to agitate determinedly for Catholic
emancipation and repeal, which should be ensured through the

use of moral persuasion. And concluding with an appeal to Catholic and Protestant to bear with each other, using mildness and benevolence, and to mutually organize a society which

"Shall serve as a bond to its members for the purpose of virtue, happiness, liberty and wisdom by the means of intellectual opposition to grievances,"

he winds up by saying:

" Adieu, my friends ! May every sun that shines on your green island see the annihilation of an abuse, and the birth of an embryon of melioration ! Your own hearts— may they become the shrines of purity and freedom, and never may smoke to the Mammon of Unrighteousness ascend from the polluted altar of their devotion."

In a postscript to this pamphlet, he urges

" A plan of amendment and regeneration in the moral and political state of society, on a comprehensive and systematic philanthropy which shall be sure, though slow in its projects ; and as it is without the rapidity and danger of revolution, so will it be devoid of the time-servingness of temporizing reform ;"

and quotes Lafayette:

" A name endeared by its peerless bearer to every lover of the human race, 'For a nation to love liberty, it is sufficient that she knows it to be free ; it is sufficient that she wills it.'"

His other Dublin pamphlet, *A Proposal for an Association of Philanthropists*, consists of remarks of the same character as the former, but he gives a summary of the French Revolution, which he endeavors to clear from the slurs which had been cast thereon. The information has come down to us through one of Shelley's biographers, that he spoke at several meetings in Dublin. At the one in which he made his first appearance in public he aroused a large assembly to enthusiasm by his fervid eloquence, and yet, notwithstanding all his efforts, his toleration unfortunately became the great stumbling-block in his attempts on behalf of Ireland, for we learn that at another meeting of patriots :

" So much ill-will against the Protestants was shown, that Shelley was provoked to remark that the Protestants were fellow-Christians and fellow-subjects, and were therefore entitled to equal rights and equal toleration with the Papists. Of course, he was forthwith interrupted by savage yells. A fierce uproar ensued, and the denouncer of bigotry was compelled to be silent. At the same meeting, and afterward, he was even threatened with personal violence, and the police suggested to him the propriety of quitting the country."

By many it has been said that Shelley was unsuccessful in his self-imposed task, but he was simply before his time, and no wonder, when we remember the condition of Ireland at the time of his visit.

We know to-day that much of what he demanded has been conceded to Ireland by liberal English governments. An alien Church has been disestablished ; public education, Catholic emancipation, and a good deal more, has been given. In the late repeal movement, the young Ireland party, the Fenian organization, and the present Home Rule agitation, we find, as Shelley wished, Catholic and Protestant working arm in arm, their colors being an admixture of orange and green—a healthy sign.

Those who dislike this noble people — for the name is legion of those who are fond of shouting " No Irish need apply " — I would recommend to think calmly over Irish history, to remember the frightful outrages put upon this generous, warm-hearted, and impulsive race for centuries, and read up Froude, Mitchell, Goldwin-Smith, McGee, Morán, and other Irish historians.

We know what the Irish are capable of, and that in Ireland, as here, after a generation or two of education, the old theological belief becomes by a gradual process less and less strong.

On September 6th, 1819, a red letter day was added to the English calendar, through the slaughter by cavalry of a number of unarmed men, who were agitating, peaceably, for the rights of labor. This is known to posterity as the "Peterloo Massacre," and happened in Manchester, on the site of the present superb Free Trade Hall, erected by the Free Traders to commemorate the ultimate triumph of their cause over the capitalists, who, in the manufacturing districts, were, until a few years back, always aided by the military in putting down strikes or demands for increase of wages.

At the time of this outrage Shelley was in Italy ; in consequence of it his attention was concentrated more than previously on the labor question, and he immediately composed half a dozen inspiriting poems, full of the fire of genius ; in one of which he calls, with a voice of thunder, to the

I.

" Men of England ! wherefore plough
For the lords who lay ye low ?
Wherefore weave, with toil and care,
The rich robes your tyrants wear ?

II.

Wherefore feed and clothe and save,
From the cradle to the grave,
Those ungrateful drones who would
Drain your sweat—nay, drink your blood?

III.

Wherefore, bees of England, forge
Many a weapon, chain, and scourge,
That these stingless drones may spoil
The forced produce of your toil?

IV.

Have ye leisure, comfort, calm,
Shelter, food, love's gentle balm?
Or what is 't ye buy so dear
With your pain, and with your fear?

V.

The seed ye sow, another reaps ;
The wealth ye find another keeps ;
The robes ye weave, another wears ;
The arms ye forge, another bears.

VI.

Sow seed—but let no tyrant reap ;
Find wealth—let no impostor heap ;
Weave robes—let not the idle wear ;
Forge arms—in your defence to bear.

VII.

Shrink to your cellars, holes, and cells ;
In halls ye deck, another dwells.
Why shake the chains ye wrought ? Ye see
The steel ye tempered, glance on ye !

VIII.

With plough and spade, and hoe and loom,
Trace your grave, and build your tomb,
And weave your winding sheet, till fair
England be your sepulchre !"

By far the finest composition brought out by this occasion
was the "Masque of Anarchy," a magnificent poem of ninety-
one verses. "Anarchy" he describes as riding "on a white
horse,"* in alliance with theology and statecraft, and whose admirers were "lawyers and priests."

---

* This doubtless alludes to the House of Hanover, the principal charge on whose
armorial bearings is a white horse.

After a series of powerful delineations, he describes slavery and freedom, justice, wisdom, peace and love, in exquisite terms. Then he turns to their lamps—science, poetry, and thought, which make secure "the lot of the dwellers in the cot."

He advises—That, on some spot of English ground, should be convened a great assembly of the fearless and the free, who shall come from the bounds of the English coast, and from every hut, village, and town, where, for other's misery and their own, they live, suffer, and moan. Also,

> "From the workhouse and the prison,
>   Where, pale as corpses newly risen,
>   Women, children, young and old,
>   Groan for pain, and weep for cold;

> "From the haunts of daily life,
>   Where is waged the daily strife
>   With common wants and common cares,
>   Which sow the human heart with tares."

When face to face with their oppressors, no force should be used, but instead

> "strong and simple words,
>   Keen to wound as sharpened swords,
>   And wide as targes let them be,
>   With their shade to cover ye."

The description of the Peterloo massacre which follows, is one of the finest pieces of composition in the language, and the poem concludes by calling the "Men of England, Heirs of Glory, Heroes of Unwritten Story," to

> "Rise like lions after slumber
>   In unvanquishable NUMBER!
>   Shake your chains to earth, like dew
>   Which in sleep had fall'n on you;
>   'YE ARE MANY—THEY ARE FEW.'"

In a pamphlet, written ostensibly on the death of the Princess Charlotte, he calls attention to the fact that three men had been executed in the interests of the "big-hearted and generous capitalists," of whom we now-a-days hear so much from their interested admirers, but whose wings are now fortunately clipped.

Shelley considered that there was no real wealth but man's labor, and that speculators pandering to selfishness, the twin-sister of debased theology, took a pride in the production of useless articles of luxury and ostentation. Imbued with this spirit, a man of wealth imagines himself a patriot when employing laborers on the erection of a mansion, or a woman of fashion indulging in luxurious dress, fancies she is aiding the laboring poor. He observes of such instances as these :

"Who does not see that this is a remedy which aggravates, whilst it palliates the countless diseases of society? The poor are set to labor—for what? Not the food for which they famish ; not the blankets for want of which their babes are frozen by the cold of their miserable hovels ; not those comforts of civilization without which civilized man is far more miserable than the meanest savage, oppressed as he is by all its insidious evils, within the daily and taunting prospect of its innumerable benefits assiduously exhibited before him ; no, for the pride of power, for the miserable isolation of pride, for the false pleasures of the hundredth part of society."

Labor is required for physical, and leisure for moral improvement. What is wanted, he considered, is a state to combine the advantages of both and have the evils of neither. In fact, any unnecessary labor which deprives the race of intellectual gain, and all times not required for the manufacture of commodities which are necessary for the subsistence of humanity, should be occupied only in mental or physical culture.

Shelley lays down as a principle that commerce is the venal interchange of what human art or nature yields, and which should not be purchased by wealth, but demanded by want. Labor and commerce, when badly regulated, scatter withering curses and open

> "The doors to premature and violent death,
> To penury, famine, and full-fed disease."

Wealth was a living God, who rules in scorn, and whom peasants, nobles, priests, and kings blindly reverence, and by whom everything is sold—the light of heaven, earth's produce, the peace of outraged conscience, the most despicable things, every object of life, and even life itself.

In a proper condition of society, which should be strictly co-operative, there would necessarily be no pauperism, and

> "No meditative signs of selfishness,
> No jealous intercourse of wretched gain,
> No balancings of prudence, cold and long ;
> In just and equal measure all is weighed ;
> One scale contains the sum of human weal,
> And one the good man's heart."

The fruits of Shelley's enunciations on the labor and capital questions, and the school of political economists to which he belonged, have made wondrous progress. The world is beginning to see that labor has the unrestricted right of coalition, that there should be only a standard day's work, according to the wants of society, with prohibition of labor for at least one day in the week ; that legislation is required for the protection of the life and health of the working man, and that mines, factories, and workshops should be strictly controlled by sanitary officers selected by labor ; that no children's work should be permitted, or women's, which may be considered unhealthy ; that prison work should be regulated, and that laborers' co-operative and benevolent societies should be administered independently of the State.

Liberals must learn from their enemies, must organize and let the ramifications of unshackled thought spread through the lands, and must, above all, conserve the control of education. Whereever there is a church or chapel, let there be beside it a hall or club, in which shall be inculcated the simple doctrines of a pure, integralised religion.

On the statute book of England there yet remains a law directed against the freedom of the press and discussion ; to even discuss the question of the divinity of Christ was considered blasphemy, and the person so offending was punished most severely by the criminal laws. At the present time this wretched remnant of the dark ages is practically a dead letter. The friends of Shelley suffered from this most intolerant spirit. Keats, it is believed by many, was wounded unto death for daring to speak on behalf of freedom, and we are given glimpses in the *Adonais* of his feelings on the subject; Leigh Hunt and his brother were imprisoned and fined for the same; the publisher of the pirated edition of Shelley's *Queen Mab* was cast into Newgate ; Eaton, a London bookseller, had been sentenced by Lord Ellenborough to a lengthened incarceration, for publishing Paine's *Age of Reason*, and hundreds of others suffered similarly. The abominable circumstance of Eaton's conviction caused great uproar; the Marquis of Wellesley, in the House of Lords, stated it was "contrary to the mild spirit of the Christian religion ; for no sanction can be found under that dispensation which will warrant a government to impose disabilities

and penalties upon any man on account of his religious opin-
ions." Shelley, who was then only nineteen years of age, and
had himself suffered from bigotry at Oxford, threw himself publicly into the controversy with great vehemence, with "a composition of great eloquence and logical exactness of reasoning,
and the truths which it contains on the subject of universal toleration are now generally admitted." Lady Shelley, from whom
I have just quoted, says that her husband's father, "from his
earliest boyhood to his latest years, whatever varieties of opinion
may have marked his intellectual course, never for a moment
swerved from the noble doctrine of unbounded liberty of thought
and speech. To him the rights of intellect were sacred ; and all
kings, teachers, or priests who sought to circumscribe the activity of discussion, and to check by force the full development of
the reasoning powers, he regarded as enemies to the independence of man, who did their utmost to destroy the spiritual
essence of our being."

To Shelley's able advocacy, and to his appeals against the
stamping out of political and social truths opposed to custom,
particularly the celebrated letter to Lord Ellenborough, it cannot be denied that the toleration now enjoyed in Great Britain
owes much.

Shelley was one of those who most earnestly deprecated punishment by death. In his early years, if a man stole a sheep,
or shot a hare, committed forgery or larceny, was a recusant
catholic or a wizard, there was, on his conviction, but one pen-
alty meted out—death. To Shelley's sensitive nature, this
painted and tinged everything around him with an aspect of
blood. In one of his political pamphlets, summoning all his
energies, he depicts in fearful colors, the depraved example of
an execution—how it brutalized the race, and how it was the duty
of man not to commit murder on his fellow-man, in the name
of the laws. The abolition of the first of these, he stated that
reformers should propose on the eve of a great political change.
He considered that the punishment by death harbored revenge and
retaliation, which legislation should be the means of eradica-
ting, and he urged that

"Governments which derive their institutions from the existence of circumstances of barbarism and violence, with some rare exceptions, perhaps, are bloody in proportion as they
are despotic, and form the manners of their subjects to a sympathy with their own spirit."

In England, as in many other countries, capital punishment is now only employed on conviction of murder or high treason. In Spain and Italy it was totally abolished, on the foundation of their young republics. Thus have the labors of Shelley, and other reformers for the good of humanity, aided to extinguish crime made law.

Cruelty to animals was another reform agitated by Shelley. His love for the animal kingdom and hatred of blood-shedding, was so great, that he personally carried the passion to such an extent as to become a vegetarian, and endeavored to induce others to be the same, in an admirable argument of some length in the notes to "Queen Mab."

The subject of the Rights of Women is approached and expatiated on, perhaps learnedly, by individuals utterly incompetent to deal with the question. Such persons, frequently armed with Sunday-school platitudes, believing in the inferiority of women, consequent on the supposed fall, and doubtless with heads paved with good intentions, as a certain place is said to be, do more harm than good to the cause. This is not wanted, and is worse than useless. To found a real republic on a solid basis, it can be legislated for only by removing the ancient landmarks by a gradual process, and coming face to face with a new order of things, without bias or prejudice borrowed from the past. Thus that noble woman, Mary Wolstonecraft, as well as John Stuart Mill, Percy Bysshe Shelley, and numerous others, have treated this all-important question, which cannot be shirked by the race. True reformers ask: What was the condition of the sex in the past? Look down the revolving cycles and note. In ancient Egypt, woman in the upper classes was almost the equal of man, and although, like Cleopatra, she could wield the sceptre, yet in the lower her condition was wretched; in Asia, a mere slave and object of Zenana lust; in savagedom, a beast of burthen. In Rome and Greece, Shelley shall tell the story:

" Among the ancient Greeks the male sex, one half of the human race, received the highest cultivation and refinement; whilst the other, so far as intellect is concerned, were educated as slaves, and were raised but few degrees in all that related to moral or intellectual excellence above the condition of savages. * * * The Roman women held a higher consideration in society, and were esteemed almost as the equal partners with their husbands in the regulation of domestic economy and the education of their children."

Regard the incidents of a Jewish wooing, in which the woman

had no voice, and of the marriage, the infernal punishments for adultery, and the accounts of the seraglios of the Hebrew kings equalled only by Turkish harems, and some of the passages in the inspired Book of Numbers, for instance, in which the horrible truth is frequently too evident, and only equalled by the fact that after lust had played out its passion, unfortunate women, taken in captivity, could, by divine command, be turned adrift to rot or starve. In Christian Feudalism we find nothing much better. If I have read history correctly, and I may be wrong— the upper-grade women in mediæval Europe, who were adored, not with love, but with lascivious and sensual worship, by Christian knights and troubadours, and who, like criminals to the halter, were forced, rarely with their own consent, into the arms of men they disliked or had never seen, or were placed in conventual houses against their wills. Of the lower-grade women, I need only offer one example—and that is sufficient to-show their awful degradation ; the French and German feudal lord had the right of *cuissage*, or, in plain English, the embraces of his serf-retainer's bride on the marriage night.

Shelley considered that in consequence of all this, men had forgotten their duties to the other sex, and that even at the time at which he lived woman was still in great social bondage, improperly educated, tied down by restrictions, and refused participation in the higher positions of labor. He called not in vain, against the inequality of the sexes, and asserted that woman's position must and should be altered by forgetting the tyranny of the past, and, be determined, for the good of the future.

We should be rejoiced that eloquent exponents of the abominations of former ages, the evils of the present, and the proper position of the future, are now hard at work. The "Women's Rights" party is up teaching men their duties on every continent ; in distant India, the Brahmo Somaj is battling, not vainly, against the horrors of the Zenana, and in conservative England, which has been stormed, and the forlorn hope is now taking possession of the citadel ; everywhere it is the same. Yes, woman, thanks to Shelley and the reformers, is about to be emancipated and free ; free to earn her living, how, where, and when she likes ; the equal of man, who shall no longer play such fantastic tricks as he did in the past, in proof of his dignity and superiority. The fourth of July is not long past and gone; I trust that in the dim vista of the future, our descendants will keep a national holiday, or a day to be set apart on which shall be celebrated the "Declaration of the Independence of Women," and then, perhaps, Shelley's description of woman in the "Episychidion" will be more apparent:

> " Seraph of heaven! too gentle to be human,
> Veiling beneath the radiant form of woman
> All that is unsupportable in thee,
> Of light, and love, and immortality."

I now approach a very delicate portion of my essay: the question of the marriage relation. By many it is scouted with much virtuous indignation, but I conceive that the liberal, who, like too many, dare not discuss this matter in its broadest and widest aspects, should be stigmatized as unworthy of the name. Christ is reported to have urged the admirers of his ethical system to take up their cross and follow him, leaving father, mother, wife, children, and all they may have—thus Shelley acted, and it bears as equally pregnant lessons to free thinkers as it did to those Syrian fishermen. Oh, that liberals had as much "faith" in the truth, in the efficacy of their cause, as the first Christians are said to have had in the teachings of that Christ whom they regarded not as a Divinity, but as a son of God, as we to-day are sons of God, of the most high! Oh, that we could carry that "faith" into our beliefs, and the determination to be stopped at no obstacle which may bar the progress of truth, which must conquer in the end!

The favorite theme in the writings of Shelley is "Eros," love of the individual, of the race, of nature, and in this he follows Christ, in whose system of Philosophy, Love is ever the predominating idea which permeates mankind with its beneficial effects, and will, when the bastard tinsel with which the truths of the Nazarene are hidden, be replaced by that pure gold which it is impossible to trace in the enunciations of any previous philosopher. This subject is always present to Shelley, and he thus appeals in one of his poems to the

> " Great Spirit, deepest Love!
> Which rulest and dost move
> All things which live, and are."

In another place he inquires—

"What is love? Ask him who lives, what is life? Ask him who adores, what is God?"

And in the same essay he describes love as

"The bond and sanction which connects man with man, and with everything which exists."

Elsewhere he points out that the attainment of love

"urges forth the power of man to arrest the faintest shadow of that without the possession of which there is no rest nor respite to the heart over which it rules, (and that) so soon as this want or power is dead, man becomes the living sepulchre of himself, and what yet survives is the mere husk of what once he was."

Of such was Shelley's philosophy of love, and I would ask if it be conceivable that the abominable calumny prompted by theological virus, that he kept a seraglio, as his friend Leigh Hunt informs us was reported, had any real existence. Shelley was too pure for any such idea as that of promiscuous sexual intercourse to be acted on by himself; his life, which lies open before us, refutes the diabolical invention. The fact was, that at the early age of nineteen he married Harriet Westbrook, the daughter of a retired tavern keeper, a woman without soul and that congeniality of disposition which a man overflowing with the pulses of genius should have chosen. After a wretched existence without intellectual sympathy, and on the advice of her father, who did not agree with his ideas on religion, they parted by mutual consent, never to meet again. Shelley about this period met his second wife, a woman of the highest powers of mind and charm of body, Mary Wolstonecraft Godwin, the authoress of *Frankenstein* and other works, daughter of William Godwin, the novelist, and author of *Political Justice* and Mary Wolstonecraft, the gifted writer of *The Rights of Women*. We are told by Lady Shelley that, "To her, as they met one eventful day in St. Pancras churchyard, by her mother's grave, Bysshe, in burning words, poured forth the tale of his wild past, how he had suffered, how he had been misled, and how, if supported by her love, he hoped, in future years, to enroll his name with the wise and good, who had done battle for their fellowmen and been true through all adverse storms to the cause of humanity. Unhesitatingly she placed her hand in his, and linked her fortune with his own."

After the death of his first wife, on the solicitation of Godwin, who was anxious for the landed interests of his grandchildren, a *legal* union was performed. After looking on this episode, in the most charitable manner, I am confident the sternest moralist cannot but "acknowledge that the passionate love of a boy should not be held a serious blemish, in a man whose subsequent life was exceptional in virtue and beneficence."

Believing, as I have explained, in the divinity of love, Shelley regarded everything in the relation of the sexes with the most intense horror, which was not consistent with "freedom ;" and by which he most certainly did not signify the license attributed by many. When he looked around and saw the withering blast of forced marriages, conjugal hatred and prostitution, can we be astonished at his passionately exclaiming :

> " Even love is sold ; the solace of all woe
> Is turned to deadliest agony, old age
> Shivers in selfish beauty's loathing arms,
> And youth's corrupted impulses prepare
> A life of horror from the blighting bane
> Of commerce, whilst the pestilence that springs
> From unenjoying sensualism, has filled
> All human life with hydra-headed woes ?"

In a most important essay bearing on this passage, which should be widely studied, he observes :

" Love is inevitably consequent upon the perception of loveliness. Love withers under constraint ; its very essence is liberty ; it is compatible neither with obedience, jealousy, nor fear ; it is then most pure, perfect, and unlimited, where its votaries live in confidence, equality, and unreserve."

He then urges :

" A husband and wife ought to continue so long united as they love each other. Any law which should bind them to cohabitation for one moment after the decay of their affection, would be a most intolerable tyranny, and the most unworthy of toleration ; and there is nothing *immoral* in this separation, for love is free. To promise forever to love the same woman, is not less absurd than to promise to believe the same creed."

He states categorically that

" The present system of constraint does no more, in the majority of instances, than make hypocrites or open enemies. Persons of delicacy and virtue, unhappily united to those whom they find it impossible to love, spend the loveliest season of their lives in unproductive efforts to appear otherwise than they are, for the sake of the feelings of their partners or the welfare of their mutual offspring; and that the early education of their children takes its color from the squabbles of the parents. They are nursed in a systematic school of ill-humor, violence, and falsehood, and the conviction that wedlock is indissoluble holds out the strongest of all temptations to the perverse. They indulge without restraint in acrimony and all the little tyrannies of domestic life, when they know that their victim is without appeal. If this connection were put on a rational basis, each would be assured that habitual ill-temper would terminate in separation, and would check this vicious and dangerous propensity."

He conceived from the re-arrangement of the marriage relation by greater facility of divorce than was to be had sixty years ago,*

"A fit and natural arrangement would result."

Shelley by no means asserts that the intercourse would be promiscuous, but on the contrary believed that from the relation of parent to child a union is generally of longer duration, placed on such a footing, and marked above all others with generosity and self-devotion.

We are on the eve of great religious changes, which must consequently disturb all the social relations. Historical Christianity still holds to her old text, of marriage being a sacrament, and therefore indissoluble. The founder of Comtism developing this dogma, urges that after the death of either husband or wife the duty of the survivor is not to re-marry. Great Britain and many of the American States have conceded greater freedom in divorce, so as to carry out in a large measure the arguments of Shelley, while the theory of what is termed the "sovereignty of the individual" is propounded by the leaders of the free love party, as a cure for the present and former difficulties.

Whatever may be the outcome of the present widespread discussions I know not, but I have belief in the supreme intelligence and in humanity, and am certain that neither the home nor the race will suffer, but that out of all this agitation will come more refined sentiment and truer morality.

I must now conclude. It has been said that there are two things in which the professors of all theologies have agreed— "To persecute all other sects, and plunder their own." Shelley, who subscribed to no theology, was persecuted by them during his entire life, but he ever forgave his persecutors, who he was confident acted through ignorance of his real motives, and he tells us :

---

* It should be remembered that in Shelley's day divorce was obtainable by the most wealthy only, at an enormous cost and by a lengthy process, precluding the slightest opportunity for the middle and poorer classes to avail themselves thereof.

" I have thought to appeal to something in common and unburden my inmost soul to them. I have found my language misunderstood, like one in a distant and savage land. The more opportunities they have afforded me for experience, the wider has appeared the interval between us, and to a greater distance have the points of sympathy been withdrawn. With a spirit ill-fitted to sustain such proof, trembling and feeble through its tenderness, I have everywhere sought sympathy, and have found only repulse and disappointment."

Do *we* misunderstand him? I think not, and William Howitt, a representative of the people, shall answer for them : " For liberty of every kind he was ready to die. For knowledge, and truth, and kindness, he desired only to live. He was a rare instance of the union of the finest moral nature and the finest genius. If he erred, the world took ample revenge upon him for it, while he conferred in return his amplest blessing on the world. It was long a species of heresy to mention his name in society ; that is passing fast away. It was next said that he never could become popular, and therefore the mischief he could do was limited. He *has* become popular, and the good he is likely to do will be unlimited. The people read him, though we may wonder at it, and they comprehend him."

This estimate is not overrated, for, having confidence in his mission to humanity, he was fortified by the belief of his existing as an indestructible portion of interminable nature and the universal mind, which in all high intelligences lives through the ages, not only in the individual consciousness of the spirit, but in that immortality of soul or mind, which lives in the race.

He hated the superstitions of Christian Fetishism and tyranny over the intellect, but loved Christ and the other philosophers with a genuine affection ; he loved humanity, and was ever fond of examining its highest phases, as, for instance, through the doctrines of perfect equality in the sexes—yet he recognised that sudden changes were prejudicial before sufficient progress had been accomplished. "To destroy, you must replace." Justice he considered the sole guide, reason and duty the only law. His morality was not that of pharasaical tartuffes, nor of prudish knickerbockers, who with wide phylacteries, sit in the high places to be seen of men. He only combatted evil principles and fought hard in favor of good.

He has been quoted as being too transcendental ; he may be to dullards with imperfect reasoning faculties, or theologians, who only see through fanatical and green-monsterish spectacles, but to men who have a *live* philosophy equally adapted to modern as well as ancient thought, he is as clear as the noon-day sun. All that is required to comprehend Percy Bysshe Shelley, is integralism of that high order which has ever believed in the ultimate perfectibility of human nature, and looked "forward to a period when a new golden age would return to earth, when all the different creeds and systems of the world would be amalgamated into one, crime disappear, and man, freed from shackles, civil and religious, bow before the throne 'of his own awless soul,' or 'of the power unknown,' " whose veil it is the ambition of theosophy to raise for humanity, and remain the "inscrutable" no longer.

I have completed my task, and with humility I make the statement, knowing that before me are many who could have performed it as completely as I have crudely. I look upon my essay, in which I have treated my subject popularly, with intention, as a beacon, whence a little light may be shed dimly, hoping that others, better qualified, will bring you face to face with the full rays.

I have shown you Shelley in his writings, his life and poetry, only where they trench on his philosophical and reform ideas— I could have related to you much about his inflexibly moral, generous, and unselfishly benevolent character—his pure, gentle and loveable existence—his utter abnegation of self, learnt from the hermetic philosophy, and his despisal of transitory legislative honors—how he, the heir to thousands of dollars annually, and a baronetage, threw aside pecuniary considerations for love of the truth and benevolence, * and how, therefrom, he was often nearly dying of hunger in the streets. I could have treated him simply as a poet, full of experienced impetuosity, subtlety of expression, and precision of verse, but I have aimed to exhibit one side of his immortality to you, which lives in and by the race, for humanity.

---

* "In his heart there was nothing depraved or unsound ; those who had opportunities of knowing him best, tell us that his life was spent in the contemplation of nature. in arduous study, or in acts of kindness and affection. A man of learning, who shared the poverty so often attached to it, enjoyed from him at one period a pension of a hundred pounds sterling a year, and continued to enjoy it till fortune rendered it superfluous To another man of letters, in similar circumstances, he presented fourteen hundred pounds ; and many other acts like these are on record to his immortal honor. Himself a frugal and abstemious ascetic, by saving and economising, he was able to assist the industrious poor—and they had frequent cause to bless his name."—*National Magazine.*

Cut short in the youth of manhood, who can tell what Percy Bysshe Shelley might not have become, living for us even perhaps at this moment? What need we care, though, for does not the "Empire of the dead increase of the living from age to age?" Shelley's terrestrial body may have been cast up by the waves on the lonely Italian shore, in sweet companionship with the souls of Keats and Sophocles. His mundane elements, purified through the fire, may have returned to their kindred elements, and been

> " made one with Nature, where is heard
> His voice in all her music, from the moan
> Of thunder to the song of night's sweet bird;
> He is a presence to be felt and known,
> In darkness and in light, from herb and stone,
> Spreading itself where'er that Power move,
> Which has withdrawn his being to its own ;
> Which wields the world with never-wearied love,
> Sustains it from beneath, and kindles it above."

His cinereal ashes may lie beneath the cypresses, near the dust of the "Adonais" of his muse, under Roman sod, and where he said :

> " To see the sun shining on its bright grass, and hear the whispering of the wind among the leaves of the trees, which have overgrown the tomb of Cestius, and the soil which is stirring in the sun-warm earth, and to mark the tombs, mostly of women and young children, who, buried there, we might, if we were to die, desire a sleep they seem to sleep."

All this may have happened, but why need we repine, for as eternal as the sea, as infinite as Nature, and as the phœnix, he revivifying lives, transmigrated and transfused into humanity, for with certainty we know that

> " He lives, he wakes—'tis Death is dead, not he."

Immortal amid immortals, his spirit in communion with the Most High, fully conscious in its individuality—immortal amid mortals, his place need never be refilled, for he stands betwixt the old and the new—immortal amid the sons of song, do poets still breathe his divine afflatus—immortal amid philosophers and the regenerators of the race, with Buddha, with Moses, with Socrates, with Mahomet, with Christ—immortal amid the noble, the virtuous, the good, the wise—immortal as when living here, for from spirit-spheres we hear him bidding us repeat :

" Nor let us weep that our delight is fled
 Far from these carrion-kites that scream below ;
He wakes or sleeps with the enduring dead ;
 Thou canst not soar where he is sitting now.
Dust to the dust ! but the pure spirit shall flow
 Back to the burning fountain whence it came,
A portion of the Eternal, which must glow
 Through time and change, unquenchably the same,"

  * * * * * * * *

"Peace ! peace ! he is not dead, he doth not sleep—
 He hath awaken'd from the dream of life—
'Tis we, who, lost in stormy visions, keep
 With phantoms an unprofitable strife ;
And in mad trance, strike with our spirits' knife,
 Invulnerable nothings !"

FINIS CORONAT OPUS.